WELCOME TO CAMP KILLER

CYNTHIA MURPHY

Barrington Stoke

Published by Barrington Stoke
An imprint of HarperCollins*Publishers*
Westerhill Road, Bishopbriggs, Glasgow, G64 2QT

www.barringtonstoke.co.uk

HarperCollins*Publishers*
Macken House, 39/40 Mayor Street Upper,
Dublin 1, DO1 C9W8, Ireland

First published in 2023

ISBN 978-1-80090-228-2

10 9 8 7 6 5 4 3

A catalogue record for this book is available from the British Library.

Printed and bound in India by Replika Press Pvt. Ltd.

For my past students.
Thank you for everything you taught me.

You're all pretty awesome.

CHAPTER 1

"Who wants to hear a ghost story?" asked Chad.

Holly laughed as a chorus of groans came from the group. They watched Chad poke the sad little campfire with a branch, but it was drizzling, normal for the north of England, and he was fighting a losing battle. Holly wanted to tell Chad there was no point, but he was her new boss, and she didn't want to appear rude.

Fionn spoke up instead. "Chad, mate, I think we all just want to get to bed. We have a big day tomorrow." Fionn's dark fringe was plastered to their forehead in thick strands and their eyeliner more smudged than usual. "Unless you want to hear a *real* ghost story, that is?" Fionn asked. "About this place?"

"I do!" Rich squealed, his mouth full of melted marshmallow. "I knew this place had to be haunted as soon as we got here. I mean, there's a suit of armour on the main staircase!"

"I'm afraid that's not original," said Chad. "Just for decoration."

"Listen up then," Fionn said, rubbing their hands together. They clearly relished the way the rest of the group leaned in, looking forward to the story. The fire crackled weakly and Holly stared into the gloomy flames, waiting for Fionn to start. "Once upon a—"

"Wait!" Rich bellowed, jumping to his feet. The group groaned.

"What is it now?" Fionn said, rolling their eyes.

"I need a jumper," Rich explained. "Back in a tick!" He ran over to his cabin and the group started laughing. Rich had taken the spotlight off Fionn, who looked furious.

Holly glanced around the chattering group as they waited for Rich to come back. There were eight counsellors in all, and their boss, Chad. Chad had worked in American summer camps for years and he'd stayed in touch with some of the

British students who had worked at the camps during their summer holidays.

When Chad had the idea to start a similar business in the UK, he had contacted the former students and invited their teenage kids to come and work with him at Camp Miller. Holly had been delighted when her mum told her about the job – not only was she going to earn some money as a camp counsellor, but the whole thing just sounded like fun.

They had been doing some training so they could run the various activities, including archery, rock climbing and kayaking. So far it had all been a bit of a laugh, but things were about to get serious as the first kids arrived tomorrow. Holly wondered if the other counsellors were feeling as nervous as she was.

They were paired up into cabins and she went through a list in her head. Cabin one – Brianna and Ava. Brianna was the most organised person Holly had ever met, and Holly was *organised*. Ava didn't say much, but she constantly fidgeted with a small rose quartz crystal that was currently reflecting the light from the fire. She seemed like a bundle of anxiety, but apparently she was training for the Olympics. Holly thought that would make anyone anxious.

Cabin two was home to Grayson and Ismail. They both seemed nice and had a gentle sense of humour – Holly knew the kids would love their daft jokes. Cabin four was Fionn and Rich. Holly looked at Fionn, always cool and collected, and tried not to feel totally intimidated by them. Rich was tall and skinny and generally over the top about everything. He and Fionn probably drove each other crazy in that cabin.

That just left cabin three. Holly shared it with Emma, the messiest person alive. Holly wondered what her fellow counsellors all thought of her, then decided she didn't care. Her dad had once said Holly's name suited her because she was pretty but spiky. She still didn't know if that was supposed to be a compliment.

Rich re-joined the group, settling down on one of the benches. "That's better. You may continue."

"Give me a second," Fionn said, and made a big deal of picking up one of the long wooden skewers. They stabbed a bloated white marshmallow with the pointy end, holding it over the fire without saying anything. A few of the other counsellors giggled as the silence grew uncomfortable.

"Does anyone know the history of this place?" Fionn finally asked. A few people shrugged and some shook their heads. "Well, back in—"

"Wait, I know!" someone interrupted, a hand waving from the other side of the fire. Holly grimaced as Fionn narrowed their eyes at the hand's owner, Brianna.

Holly was starting to get a bit fed up with Brianna, the Lead Counsellor and general know-it-all.

"It was a rhetorical question," Fionn said coolly.

It was obvious Fionn was just as fed up. Brianna's cheeks flushed in the firelight and her hand sank slowly as Fionn continued.

"As I was saying, back in the 1800s, this place was somebody's home." Fionn gestured towards the building that loomed over them. It was a greying mansion, built from local stone, and their camp was situated at the back of the house, in what used to be the gardens. "This super-rich dude, John Miller, built it for his wife, Dorothea.

She wanted a gothic mansion and the man delivered – towers, a secret rose garden, the lot."

"So, what's the ghost story?" Grayson demanded, sitting up straight and stretching his arms behind him.

He was sitting so close that Holly couldn't help staring at his muscular arms that peeked out beneath the sleeves of his green Camp Miller polo shirt. She felt her cheeks grow warm at the thought of sitting by the fire with just him. Holly refocused on Fionn, hoping no one had noticed her blushing.

"It starts up there," Fionn went on. "Can you see the platform around the top of the tower?" They pointed up to the sky and every head around the campfire turned to look. "That's the Widow's Walk."

It was still light, but the building was tall and the black iron railings around the platform were hard to see against the grey sky.

Fionn continued, "Anyway, John Miller built Dorothea this house, complete with the Widow's Walk she wanted. He was some kind of spice merchant, sailing around the world on a huge ship, the kind you'd see on *Pirates of the*

Caribbean. Dorothea asked for a walkway on top of the highest tower, where she could go and look out to sea when John was due to return. A classic tale, right? Lonely wife sadly awaits return of husband."

"What happened to Dorothea?" Brianna whispered, and goosebumps prickled Holly's arms. The rest of the group were quiet, entranced.

"Well, one day she climbed up the tower and onto the Widow's Walk," said Fionn. "John was due back that week and Dorothea spent hours up there, waiting and hoping for him to return. Up until this trip, he'd always made it home."

"So, he didn't come back?" Rich whispered.

"Oh, John came back," Fionn said. They watched the edges of the marshmallow turn brown as they twisted it over the fire. "But this time, he wasn't alone."

"Damn," Holly said, leaning back from the fire. "He didn't bring back another woman?"

"Worse." Fionn twisted their skewer and pushed it further into the flames. "He brought back a woman *and* their newborn son. Dorothea had never been able to have children, so John had looked elsewhere for an heir to his fortune. What a guy, right? He expected them all to live together – the mother of his child would work as a housekeeper and Dorothea would raise their baby as her own. Can you imagine?"

"No," Brianna said softly. "That's awful."

"So did Dorothea do it?" Grayson asked. "Look after the kid?"

"Hell no. The situation sent her mad. John and his new family were found dead, and then some hunters came across Dorothea's body in the woods, by her beloved rose garden. She had crawled out there in her white nightgown, her legs mangled and broken. The legend goes that Dorothea was holding her own funeral flowers – red roses from her garden. There are locals who say she still haunts the place. That the house is cursed."

"Creepy," said Ava, who shuddered in the seat next to Grayson.

"Wait," Grayson said, furrowing his brow. "You said 'John and his new family were found dead'. You mean the other woman? And the kid?"

Fionn nodded.

"Wait," whispered Brianna. "Even the baby?"

"Yep."

"What happened?" Ava whispered.

Fionn finally pulled their marshmallow from the fire, pointing the flaming lump of sugar up to the top of the tower. "The legend says that Dorothea set the house on fire and jumped off the Widow's Walk."

CHAPTER 2

"Well, I think that's time for bed, folks!" Chad said, jumping to his feet. He picked up a bucket of sand, scooping handfuls out and dumping them on the flames. Another chorus of groans followed. The poor man was getting his own soundtrack. "And don't be telling the kids that story when they arrive tomorrow, all right?" Chad added. "We don't want them crying themselves to sleep with thoughts of ghosts and burning houses."

"I am definitely telling *my* kids," Grayson whispered to Holly. "Might start calling it 'Camp *Killer*' instead, to keep them in line."

Holly giggled, her cheeks burning while she watched the other counsellors begin to stand up and stretch. She studied Grayson out of the corner of her eye, not wanting to be too obvious. He really was cute, but he hadn't shown much interest in her.

Until now.

"Are you going back to your cabin?" Holly asked him, brushing her long auburn hair back as she got to her feet.

Chad was tidying up the remains of their campfire, waving away offers of help from the others.

"Yeah, it looks like Ismail's already gone," Grayson said. He stood up and brushed tiny splinters from the log seat off his trousers.

"Looks like my roomie's gone too," Holly said. She hadn't even noticed that Emma had left. Emma was not only messy but boring, a timid little girl who huffed and groaned when Holly was doing basic things like moisturising before bed. "Ismail seems nice."

"Yeah, he's pretty cool, apart from the fact that our room is full of his trainers. I swear he brought a different pair for every day of the week."

"I hope he doesn't expect them to last the summer. They'll get ruined here in no time," Holly laughed.

"Night, Chad," Grayson called.

Holly waved as they started to walk away.

"Sleep well," Chad replied, swinging a black bin liner in a wave. "Big day tomorrow!"

"Are you nervous?" Holly asked Grayson. The walk from the firepit to the cabins at the edge of the trees was a short one, but it was getting much darker and everything was draped in shadow.

"A bit," Grayson admitted, his feet crunching over the loose gravel. "It's a big responsibility, you know?"

"Yeah, I guess. But I have three younger siblings, so it can't be much different than looking after them."

"No, I guess not. Four of you at home then? That's cool."

"Sometimes," Holly said. "What about you?"

"Only child," Grayson replied as they reached Holly's cabin. The cabins were large wooden A-frame buildings that had been built for Camp Miller. "It can be lonely, but my parents are OK, I guess."

"That's good." Holly climbed the porch steps and turned to face Grayson. Neither of them spoke. Awkward.

"Night, Holly." He smiled at her, flashing his straight white teeth in the gloom. She could just make out his wire retainer.

"Night, Grayson," Holly said, giving a little wave as he walked over to his cabin. Had he just walked her home? Cute.

Holly lingered on the porch for a moment, gazing up towards the Widow's Walk. The rear entrance to the house was opposite her cabin, the firepit in between. She shuddered at the gaping mouth of the back door. It looked as if it was leering at her, the two blank windows like eyes above it. She hoped Fionn's little story had been just that – a story.

Camp Killer.

Holly rubbed the goosebumps that had sprung up on her bare arms again and turned her back to the house, pressing the code into the keypad next to the cabin door. Chad might be an over-cheery American, but at least his focus on security meant she felt safe sleeping out here.

Holly entered the main room of the cabin. It was lined with tall, skinny metal lockers, one for each child, and there were four sets of bunkbeds that would be full of ten and eleven year olds tomorrow. She was so glad the counsellors had their own separate room with a window at the side of the cabin – even if she did have to share it with Emma.

"Hey, Emma," Holly said as she pushed open the door to their room.

Emma was already in bed, covers pulled up over her chin, headphones and eye mask firmly in place, only a tiny bit of her freckled skin visible. She didn't move. At least she'd left the lights on for Holly this time.

Holly opened the small wardrobe at the end of her bed. Five washed and pressed Camp Miller polo shirts hung there, forest green and ready for the week ahead. A selection of dull beige shorts and cargo pants hung next to them, along with a Camp Miller hoodie and a plain black waterproof jacket. Holly sighed, thinking of her jeans and summer dresses back home. Her denim shorts. She couldn't wait to get dressed up at the end of this summer season.

Holly leaned down to unlace the hiking boots she was required to wear. She eased them off, placing them in the bottom of the wardrobe and throwing her socks in the collapsible laundry basket she kept in there. She slid her feet into flip-flops and tied her hair into a bun. She grabbed her towel and shower basket from the top shelf, closed the wardrobe and collected pyjamas from beneath her pillow. She tried not to look at the mess Emma had left – clothes all over their shared dressing table, balled-up socks and a damp towel decorating the floor. Holly shuddered. How was she going to live with this girl for four whole weeks?

Holly closed the bedroom door and turned on the lights in the main room. For some reason the bathrooms were at the back of the cabin – her mum had warned her about this from her trip to the American camp, but Holly had hoped it might be different here. Maybe they'd even have an en-suite, but no such luck. She would have to creep through the kids' room every time she wanted to go to the loo. At least the toilets weren't outside.

When she reached the bathroom, Holly sighed. This would be her last peaceful shower for the next month. She entered a shower cubicle and cranked the handle all the way around, shedding her uniform as the water began to steam slightly. She hung her towel on a hook and carefully placed her shower basket on the floor, making sure none of her hair had escaped from the bun.

She was just about to step into the warm water when the yelling started.

CHAPTER 3

"What the hell was that?" Holly shouted, running out of the cabin. She could see Brianna standing on the porch of cabin one, staring into the woods. Holly glanced the same way but could see nothing but trees. When Brianna looked over, Holly was hit by the sudden realisation that she had run out wrapped in nothing but a white towel.

"It came from in there," Brianna called back quietly, pointing at the cabin between them.

Grayson's cabin.

Holly watched as Brianna padded down her porch steps, towards the sound. Brianna threw a final look behind her, making Holly wonder what she was searching for in the trees. There was nothing but darkness there now.

A miserable groan from inside cabin two snapped Holly back to the present.

Brianna jogged the rest of the way over, her ponytail swishing, and Holly wished she hadn't hurried out. She wasn't leaving this porch in only a towel for anybody.

"Grayson?" Brianna called, hesitating at the bottom of the steps. "Ismail?"

"Out of the way!" a voice called from inside.

Holly wrapped her hands tightly around her porch's wooden rail. Brianna stumbled back towards the firepit as Ismail burst out of the door and threw a bundle of sheets down the steps.

"What on earth is going on out here?" Chad's voice echoed across the site, and Holly glanced around at the other cabins. There was at least one counsellor on each porch, watching the commotion: Rich was out on cabin four's and Ava had appeared on the porch she shared with Brianna. It looked like Brianna was the only one who had run towards the scream.

"Someone has a sick sense of humour, that's what's going on," said Grayson as he emerged from the cabin looking pale. His mouth was set in a tight line as he raised a shaking hand and pointed at the bundle Ismail had thrown down the stairs.

"Honestly," Chad huffed, marching over to lift the white sheet off the ground. "What is it?"

It moved.

"What the …?" Holly whispered as Chad dropped the sheet. A knotted mass of thick, muscular bodies began to writhe and curl out of the bundle and onto the ground. A rotten smell followed them and Holly wrinkled her nose.

"Snakes!" Brianna squealed, and clambered onto one of the logs around the firepit. The snakes were winding around something that had fallen from the sheet with them. Holly squinted. Were they … flowers? No, not just flowers. Roses.

Red roses.

Holly watched the snakes twist around the stems and became very aware of her bare legs. She could almost feel the snakes coiling around her ankles.

"Someone put them in my bed," Grayson shouted, shaking his arms out as if the snakes were on him. "I got in it! I climbed under the covers without turning on the lights and … and …" He stopped, looking as if he was trying not to vomit.

Holly shivered at the thought and inched back towards her cabin door.

"It's fine – they're just grass snakes," Fionn said, appearing from the treeline and walking towards the writhing mound. "They're not poisonous, and they're definitely more scared than you are right now – that's why they stink. It's a defence mechanism." Fionn peered at the ground. "These are small – only babies."

"Wait," Brianna said, and pointed to the dark patch of trees Fionn had emerged from. "Where have you been?"

Ah, Holly thought, *so it must have been Fionn that Brianna had spotted in the woods before.*

"Here, I'll get rid of them," Fionn said, ignoring the question. They joined Chad, picking up one of the escapees with a gentle finger and thumb.

The sun had set, but in the dusk Holly could see the snake's rapidly darting tongue, its green and yellow markings. It was easily the length of her forearm – and that was only a baby? She shuddered as Fionn handled it gently and placed it back into the sheet.

"See? They're harmless," Fionn said.

The process was repeated until all the snakes were wrapped in the cloth and Fionn joined the corners together like a giant sack. "I'll put them out near the lake – they like the damp. I just need to get my lanyard with the keys from my cabin."

"Take mine," Chad said, handing over the keys that would unlock the gate to the lake area. "Thank you, Fionn."

"Sure," Fionn replied, and disappeared through the gate at the side of the house as everybody watched in silence.

Holly shuddered. *Babies. Yeah, right.*

She hoped Fionn had collected them all.

"I want everyone to listen very carefully," Chad said, his voice serious. He walked to the firepit so he could look at each of the cabins in turn. "We don't have time for pranks. Whoever did this was way out of order and if they do anything like this again—"

"Again?" Grayson groaned. "You mean you're letting whoever did this get away with it? I got into *bed* with those things."

Chad held up a hand to silence Grayson, and Holly noticed that her boss's jaw was clenched tight. "Not at all. But we have thirty-two children arriving here at 8 a.m. and I don't have time to discipline my staff for practical jokes. Understood?"

Holly nodded amongst a whisper of yeses and Grayson's grumbles. The air was cold on her bare skin and she longed to sneak back inside.

"Good. Grayson, if you want to come and see me at lunch tomorrow, we can talk about it. But there was no real harm done, right?"

Grayson shrugged.

"OK. Now get back to bed, all of you. We have a long week ahead of us." Chad strode back to the main house, where his office and sleeping quarters were.

Holly went back inside the cabin for a shower, jealous that Emma had managed to sleep through the whole thing.

At least one of them wouldn't be dreaming about snakes.

CHAPTER 4

The kids arrived between eight and nine the next morning. When they'd all dumped their stuff in the cabins, the counsellors took them out to sit around the firepit. The fire wasn't lit this morning, but the benches around it were full of eager little faces, all turned towards the front, where Brianna was explaining how a normal day at camp would work. She was clearly relishing her position as Lead Counsellor.

One of the kids who'd be staying in Holly's cabin sat up straight and waved excitedly at her. Holly walked over and took a seat beside her, giving the kid a little fist bump as she sat down. The girl beamed.

Brianna carried on talking and Holly made sure she at least looked like she was listening. "First there's your wake-up call and the flag raising, then we will all have breakfast together in the Great Hall. We'll have lunch in there today and your counsellors will give you a tour of the grounds after. After breakfast each morning, it's cabin clean-up."

Brianna paused, as if waiting for the kids to moan or heckle, but they were too excited. Holly smiled at her group as Brianna checked her clipboard and carried on. "Then we'll have morning activities, which you'll get a little taste of in a few minutes, followed by a picnic lunch and some afternoon activities. These could be anything from rock climbing to kayaking. You'll even get to try archery with our expert and Olympic hopeful, Ava."

A teeny girl at the front raised her hand to ask a question and Holly's attention drifted. The campground was full compared to last night. There were five large logs that acted as benches, all arranged around the firepit. Each of the four cabins had their own bench, the corresponding number painted on its rear, with space for eight kids to perch on each one, plus their counsellors at either end.

The fifth bench was for Chad and any of the other staff like the cooks or cleaners who might join them for s'mores or campfire stories.

And then there was the flagpole.

Holly found the whole flag thing weird. Chad said that in America they raised the Stars and Stripes and pledged allegiance at camp each day, whatever that meant. Here they raised a bottle-green flag with the yellow Camp Miller logo on it instead.

She zoned back into what was happening just in time to see Ava usher two little girls up to the front. These two looked much younger than ten. They were all wispy hair and knobbly knees. Holly wondered if they'd be able to hoist the flag at all.

"This is a very special part of our day," Chad told the group as he unfurled the large flag. On it was the Camp Miller logo – the yellow silhouette of a pine tree, a crescent moon and a small wolf with its snout in the air.

Not that there were any wolves in the north-west of England.

"What was that?" asked the girl next to Holly as she tugged on her sleeve.

Holly looked down into wide eyes. "What?"

"That sound. Like a big splash. Listen," she whispered.

Holly strained her ears but could only hear the kids. They were cheering on the two little girls who pulled the flag rope in tandem.

She glanced around the firepit and stood up discreetly, edging her way over to the chain-link fence that ran around the lake's perimeter. Not all the counsellors were here – Fionn wasn't on their bench and neither were Rich or Grayson, but she was sure she'd heard Rich ask Grayson to give him a hand down at the lake earlier. They were probably still setting up their activities. Brianna and her clipboard had disappeared now too, probably to do something Very Important.

Then she heard it. Another splash, like the sound an oar makes when it slaps still water. Holly narrowed her eyes, squinting to see between the rushes. Then she gasped. Was that a dark shape on the surface of the lake?

Holly pushed down her panic and walked over to Ava. She was standing to the side, cheering on the girls as Chad helped them with the flag. Holly beckoned to her and Ava hesitated before joining Holly at the edge of the circle.

"What is it?" Ava said through a smile.

Holly turned her back to the campers – she didn't want to upset the kids on their first day. "I think someone might have fallen in the lake."

Ava's face drained of colour.

"I'm not sure, but I'm going to go and check," Holly whispered. "Can you tell Chad to follow me?"

Ava nodded and Holly took off towards the gate. Once she was round the corner of the house and out of sight, she started to jog, picking up speed when her view opened up. She could see Grayson leaning over a body at the side of the lake.

He was clearly trying to resuscitate Rich, whose skin was as grey as the water.

CHAPTER 5

Rich started to sputter to life just as Holly reached them, Chad right behind. She looked on, shocked as Rich lay on the dock and clawed the air for breath. He sucked it deep into his chest as he rolled over. The edges of the wooden slats that made up the walkway creaked.

Rich was alive.

"Are you guys OK?" Holly asked as Grayson crouched next to Rich. He was soaked to the bone too.

"I think so," Rich replied, pushing himself up to sitting. His body was wracked by another round of coughs. Rich pointed a weak finger at Grayson. "You're drenched. Wait … did you …?"

"Yeah." Grayson shrugged awkwardly as Chad unfolded a small silver package from his bum bag and draped it around Rich. An emergency blanket.

"What happened?" Holly asked, looking between each of them in turn.

"Grayson saved Rich's life," Chad said. He slapped Grayson on the back and he flushed red, pushing wet hair back from his face.

"But what happened?" Holly asked again. "Did your kayak capsize or something? I thought you were pretty experienced?"

"I'm not sure," said Rich. "I'm still trying to piece it together."

"He seemed to be stuck in the kayak when I got out there," Grayson said. "I'd left him to finish testing the gear so I could run back and sit with my kids, but I heard a splash and ..."

"What do you mean?" Holly asked, but Grayson just shook his head as if he was trying to understand it himself.

"Let's get Rich back to the house and we can figure it all out then," interrupted Chad.

"Can you stand?" Holly asked.

"Yeah, I think so," Rich replied. He pushed into the ground with his arms, testing his weight, then stood up carefully. He wobbled, so Holly darted to catch him, but Grayson grabbed his arm first, keeping Rich steady.

"You're OK," Grayson said.

"Dizzy," Rich whispered. It sounded like his throat was lined with broken glass. Holly couldn't help thinking how quiet and deflated Rich seemed compared to his normal loud behaviour.

Holly ducked under Rich's other arm and he leaned on her gratefully. The trio headed back towards the house, Chad walking behind, talking into his radio. Rich began throwing up lake water after a few steps and they had to pause.

"Hey! Is everything OK? What happened?" Fionn's voice rang out from near the gate.

Holly looked up in time to see Fionn drop an oar. What were they doing? Poking at something in the reeds?

"Rich got stuck in one of the kayaks," Holly answered. "He's OK – just in shock I think."

Fionn came closer and Holly could see water dripping from a bundle in their hands.

"Dude, are you all right?" Fionn asked. "Did you nearly, like, drown?" Fionn's black-ringed eyes were as big as saucers.

Rich tried to shake his head, but it was obviously too much effort.

"None of the others are answering their radios," Chad said as he caught up with them.

Holly started to chatter as they stumbled towards the gate, more to keep herself calm than anything else. "The kids are probably on the tour now, Chad. I'm sure Brianna will have taken charge."

Chad sighed, looking slightly relieved. "I hope so," he said. "We don't need the kids to see stuff like this, especially on their first day." Chad swung open the gate for them. "I'm just glad we didn't have to call 911."

"999," Fionn corrected, their eyebrows raised. "Over here it's 999. You did know that, right?"

Holly held her breath. She'd never have the nerve to talk to an adult like that.

"Of course I did," Chad said, closing the gate and clicking the padlock into place. "Force of habit, that's all. Let's go into the house."

Grayson gently steered Rich and Holly into an open door at the side of the house and into the brew room, which was really just a small kitchen area for the staff. A worktop ran across the wall to the left, covered in bottles of cheap cordial, plastic cups and a kettle. There was a stainless-steel sink on the back wall, a door that led into the main house and a tumble dryer sitting on the right, next to a rack of Camp Miller fleeces.

"Shirt," Chad said.

Holly and Grayson stepped aside to give Rich some room. He peeled his wet top off, the fabric sucking at his skin. Rich handed it over, swapping it for the dry fleece Chad held out. Holly smiled at him as she helped him zip it up. Fionn filled the kettle and opened the cupboard to look for teabags.

"Sit," Holly directed, taking charge as if Rich was one of her little brothers.

Rich climbed up on a tall stool and slumped forwards onto the worktop. He looked warmer in the fleece, but he was clearly exhausted. His bottom half was still soaking, but Holly wasn't asking him to take his trousers off and swap them for dry ones, no chance.

"Here. It's just plain black tea. I didn't know if you took milk or sugar …" Fionn said as they placed a steaming hot travel cup in front of Rich. They headed back to the sink and started to wring out a soaking cloth.

"This is fine," Rich rasped. "Thank you."

Holly began to rummage inside the cupboards and grinned as she found the biscuits. She pushed a custard cream out of a packet with her thumb. "Here. Sugar's good for shock."

Rich took a bite and chewed, the smell of vanilla filling the small room. He finished it in two mouthfuls and wrapped his hands around the mug. Holly left the packet next to him, but he shook his head.

"My throat hurts," Rich said hoarsely.

Would it be out of order for Holly to take one of the biscuits? She'd been too nervous to eat at breakfast and her stomach grumbled loudly now.

"Sorry," she muttered.

"Go for it," Rich said, and pushed the biscuits over with a weak smile.

"Thanks." Holly bit into one, letting it melt in her mouth as she looked around. She stopped when she saw Chad and Grayson whispering in the corner. They were pointing towards the lake.

"I know I shouldn't have left the gate open," Grayson apologised.

"Hey, it's OK," Chad said. "It just can't happen again – it could have been a camper." He was trying to sound soothing, but Holly could hear exasperation in his voice too.

"I guess." Grayson pushed a hand through his hair again, his face unsure. Holly's heart went out to him.

"What are you guys talking about?" she asked.

Grayson looked over to her. "Just going over what happened before. I finished helping Rich and then headed back to join everyone for the flag thing. I heard a massive splash. I ran back and saw the kayak was overturned but no Rich. So I jumped in, but I never locked the gate."

"No," Rich said, pushing his tea away and standing up.

"Are you feeling OK?" Chad said. He walked over and placed a hand on Rich's forehead. "Maybe we do need to call 91 … 999. Or your mom, Rich, but you'll have to give me her number—"

"No!" Rich shouted. "No, I'm fine. I don't want to bother anyone," he added, much more quietly. Rich brushed Chad's hand away and shivered. "Honestly, I'm fine."

"So, what's wrong?" Holly asked, as gently as she could.

"It wasn't an accident." Rich's voice was raw, scratchy.

Holly – and everyone else – stared at him. Even Fionn stopped what they were doing at the sink.

"What do you mean?" Holly breathed.

"I don't remember it all." Rich hesitated as he reached up and gingerly touched the back of his head. "I was pulling in the last kayak when something hit my head. The next thing I knew, I was in the water. I panicked and … and I overturned and …" Rich started to sob. "I couldn't get out. Then I remember something was pressing on my chest and I was throwing up. But that bit was Grayson, helping me."

"Oh my god," Holly whispered, her eyes growing wide. "Chad …"

Chad held up a hand to silence her and Holly's cheeks grew warm.

"Rich, these are pretty serious allegations," Chad said. "Are you saying someone did this to you on purpose?"

Rich nodded. "I wasn't stuck in the kayak when Grayson got to me. I was tied in!"

"Oh boy." Chad began pacing the room as Holly wrapped Rich in a hug. "OK. Give me ten minutes and then let's all meet in the staff kit room, away from the kids," Chad continued. "I'll get a movie on in the Great Hall – the cooks can watch the kids while we have a meeting." Chad disappeared out the door without another word.

"Well, we've freaked him out." Rich laughed weakly.

"Yeah," Holly said, releasing him and studying his face. "Did someone really try to hurt you?"

"Yeah, I think so." He took a sip of tea with trembling hands. "Ouch."

"Here, try this." Fionn turned on the tap and took the mug, adding a splash of cold water.

Holly was surprised at Fionn's act of kindness, but maybe they had feelings after all.

Rich gulped the strong tea down greedily.

"Better?" she asked.

"Yeah, thanks." Rich took another gulp as Fionn stretched out the cloth they'd been wringing. Holly tilted her head as she tried to work out what it was. It didn't seem to be a tea towel, as she'd thought earlier.

"What is that?" Grayson asked.

Fionn shook out the off-white fabric and a tattered red rose dropped to the floor. "A dress?" Holly asked.

"It was floating in the lake," Fionn said. They held it up and Holly could make out the old-fashioned balloon sleeves and lacy neckline. "I fished it out."

"It looks like a costume from the kind of show my mum would watch, *Bridgerton* or something,"

Rich said. "Actually, it could be from the costume box in the hall. It looks like the kind of stuff I found when I was trying to decide which show I'd perform with the kids at the end of each week."

"Oh my god!" Fionn twirled the dress around as if they were dancing with it. "You know what this could be, right?"

"Your granny's nightdress?" Grayson tried to joke, but Holly could see he was nervous. She tried to ignore that another rose had appeared when something awful had happened.

"Not just a nightdress," Fionn said, their eyes sparkling. "What if it's *Dorothea's* nightdress?"

CHAPTER 6

Later that evening, Holly listened to the soft snoring of the girls sleeping in her cabin. Getting them to wind down had been harder than she'd expected. But once the kids were washed and in their pyjamas, they were asleep as soon as their heads hit the pillows. Holly wished for the same but didn't think sleep would come easily after today. The thought that Rich had been attacked ... well. She felt pretty uneasy about the whole thing.

Holly quietly left her cabin and heard the low buzz of the other counsellors sitting around the campfire. She knew exactly what was being discussed. Despite the horror of the morning, everyone but Rich had carried on with the afternoon activities as planned. Chad had tried to give them all a "reassuring" talk in the staff kit room on the importance of following safety rules and taking care of each other. But there had been no warnings and no investigation into who might have tied Rich into that boat. Nothing.

Holly wasn't sure if that was normal procedure, but it didn't feel right to her. She wondered if that was why everyone had gathered outside – maybe it didn't feel right to them either. She took a deep breath and tried to put a smile on her face. As she continued walking, she saw Fionn sneak out from around the side of the cabin.

"Hey," Holly said.

Fionn flinched. To Holly it was the action of someone who had been caught doing something they shouldn't have been.

"Uh, hey. What's going on?" Fionn cleared their throat awkwardly and silence hung in the air as they stared at each other.

"My kids have all nodded off, so I was going to join everyone at the campfire. What about you?" Holly asked, looking pointedly at the phone in Fionn's hand.

"Nothing," Fionn muttered. They slipped the mobile into their pocket as Holly stared.

"I didn't think we could get a signal out here," she said. "I couldn't get one so just stopped using mine after we arrived."

"Don't tell on me, yeah?" Fionn's body sagged. "I was calling my girlfriend. Well ... I'm not sure she'll be my girlfriend for much longer."

Holly wished she hadn't said anything. "Sorry to hear that," she mumbled as they headed to the firepit together. She breathed a sigh of relief when they reached the others.

"So, what's the hot goss?" Fionn asked the group as if nothing had happened.

"What do you think?" Grayson said. He pointed to Rich, who was sitting by the fire. Rich still wore the thick fleece from earlier despite the heat that Holly could feel from the flames. His body was hunched and he looked sad. Deflated. Not at all like his usual self.

"Is he OK?" Fionn asked.

"I think so," Ava said. "But can you believe Chad just glossed over the whole thing? I mean, Rich could have *died*."

"I know," Holly said. It was all so weird. Poor Rich.

She stepped over a log and settled herself next to Grayson, playing with the ends of her braid as she smiled shyly at him.

"Shall we get started?" Grayson said, and Rich nodded tentatively. Holly shared a look with Fionn, who had sat down the other side of Grayson. What had they missed?

Holly studied the counsellors in the flickering firelight. Brianna's leg bounced as she poked at the fire. Emma and Ismail were too busy knee-bumping and furtively holding hands to notice anything else, which made Holly raise her eyebrows. It was always the quiet ones. Ava was hunched into herself, her eyes dark and hooded.

"So, you all know what happened this morning?" Rich said, and Holly refocused her attention. Everyone nodded. "OK. Well, what Chad failed to mention is that someone tried to *drown me on purpose.*" Rich paused for dramatic effect and Holly tried really hard not to be irritated with him. "They knocked me out, tied me in that kayak and left me there."

"Are you serious?" Brianna paused her knee and made the sign of the cross over her chest. "Who would do that?"

"I dunno." Rich shrugged. "But they did, and it was probably someone here."

"What?" Ismail said, looking up from where he was holding Emma's hand. "But we were all here with the kids."

"Not everyone ..." Rich let his voice trail off.

"He's right," Ava said as she sat up straight. "Sorry, but you weren't here, Fionn, and neither were Brianna or Ismail."

"I was setting up the zipline for this afternoon!" Fionn burst out, their cheeks reddening. Brianna mumbled something about getting an inhaler after her talk to the kids.

"And I was sorting the climbing wall. What are you trying to say?" Ismail demanded, leaning towards Ava.

"I'm just trying to figure this out," Ava said, and pointed at Grayson. "*You* were the last one with him. Why were you even out at the lake? Wasn't your group on a hike this afternoon?"

"Well, yeah, b-but—" Grayson stumbled over his words, his face flaming.

"*I* asked Grayson to help me check the lifejackets – he's a lifeguard," Rich interrupted.

"Not the only one," Ava grumbled.

"Hey, don't forget I was the target last night," Grayson said, finding his voice. "I don't remember anyone else's bed being filled with snakes."

"Wait, let's not argue." Brianna jumped up to address the group and Ava rolled her eyes. "There are loads of other people who work here during the day. It could have been one of the adults! Have you upset any of the cleaners? A caretaker?"

"No," Rich said sulkily. "And sit down. We don't want Chad to hear you."

Brianna sank back to her seat.

"You're right," Fionn said. "It could be anyone. It could be some crazed stranger. Actually, I heard Chad on the phone when I went by his office the other day. From what I could tell it was some kind of lawyer. Sounds like the descendants of the Miller family are annoyed because this place is being used as a camp. They think they should still own it."

"You got all that from listening outside the door?" Grayson asked.

"I have a particular set of skills," Fionn said with a smirk.

"But it's been used as other stuff since they sold it, hasn't it? A school for delinquents or something?" Emma whispered shakily. Ismail put an arm around her and squeezed.

"What if it's an ex-pupil?" Brianna said, a hand flying to cover her mouth.

"Come on, calm down," Grayson said. He held his hands out, palms facing the group, clearly trying to be the voice of reason. "It hasn't been a school since the seventies or something, so it's unlikely to be an old pupil looking for revenge, not after all that time."

"There's something else," said Rich.

"What?" Brianna asked as she chewed the hair at the end of her ponytail. Holly felt a bit sorry for her – she looked so nervous.

"This." Rich unzipped his fleece and produced the nightgown that Fionn had dragged from the lake earlier. Now it was dry, green and brown filth streaked it. "Fionn found this in the lake after I was pulled out."

He passed it to Ismail, who stood up and shook it, holding it up to his body with a laugh. "What is this? A dress?" he asked.

"We think it's a nightgown. A Victorian one," Holly said, "and there was a rose wrapped up in it."

"Weird." Ismail shrugged and passed it on to the next person.

Ava.

"Oh my god, like the roses with the snakes!" Ava said as she closed her eyes. "This is hers, isn't it?" She gasped and pushed it back to Ismail. "I can feel it. It's Dorothea's!"

"Why do you think that?" Ismail laughed, but Holly didn't hear any humour in it. In fact, the circle had fallen dead silent, the only sound the snap of logs in the fire.

"I know it is," said Ava. "It's hers. What if the curse is real? What if she's doing this?"

"Oh, *please*," Fionn sputtered. "A ghost didn't bash Rich over the head and tie him into that kayak. A living, breathing person did."

"Well, you told the story," Holly fired back at them, folding her arms. "Last night. You told us all about how Dorothea haunts these woods, taking revenge forevermore. Maybe it was a cover so you could cause some chaos."

Grayson leaned back slightly, caught in the crossfire between them.

"It's just a local legend," Fionn said, throwing their hands up with exasperation. "Who knows if the story is even *true*? I was just entertaining you!"

"It *is* true," Ava whispered, her face haunted. "I'm sure of it."

Holly sighed. Brianna made the sign of the cross again and clasped her hands in prayer. Ismail and Emma were both slightly paler than they had been a few seconds before. Ava was mumbling something about a protection crystal. Holly wondered if she should do something. They were losing it.

"Fine, it's true," Fionn sighed. "Dorothea is haunting the grounds and going to kill us one by one until we get off her property. Wooooo."

"It's not funny," Rich hissed.

Fionn stopped and looked at him, their face shocked. "Seriously? You think a *ghost* attacked you?"

"I don't know," Rich wailed. "I really don't know."

"OK then," Fionn said. They stood up and stretched. "You lot can stay here and tell ghost stories, but I'm going to check on my kids and shower this joke of a day off me." Fionn turned to leave, gravel crunching beneath their feet.

Holly was about to follow when a loud crack echoed around the clearing. She spun around just in time to see the flagpole snap, the top half crashing right towards Emma's head.

CHAPTER 7

"Emma!"

Holly dived forward as everyone shouted around her. The scene unfolded in slow motion as the pole crashed down. She grabbed the flag itself, hoping to slow it, but it had gained too much momentum and instead Holly fell to the ground and landed heavily on top of it.

Holly's ears rang with Brianna's screams and the shouts of the others. She squeezed her eyes shut and mentally checked her body. She had sore ribs from landing on the pole but no other pain.

The group had fallen silent. Holly cracked one eyelid open, fearful of what she would see. For a few seconds she lay on the cold gravel, shaking and sucking in deep breaths, until a hand reached out to her. Grayson's. She grabbed it gratefully and got to her feet, fighting the urge to hold on to him.

"You tried to save me," Emma said, her voice shaking as she struggled to get the words out. She was lying on the ground behind the bench as if she'd fallen backwards, her legs still draped over it. Ismail lay next to her, his normally pristine hair a mess. Emma started sobbing. "Both of you."

"You're my roomie. I can't handle eight kids on my own," Holly tried to joke, her whole body shaking. That pole was heavy. If it had hit Emma … Holly tried not to think about what might have happened.

The group was quiet. Brianna's screams had turned to sobs and she was telling Emma she was lucky to be alive, which made the poor girl cry even harder. Ismail pulled Emma to her feet and wrapped his arms around her.

"I think Emma should go to bed," Ismail said to the group. Holly nodded as Ismail slowly guided Emma to her cabin. Her eyes were red and her breathing was still shaky. "I've got you," Holly heard Ismail whisper as he led her away.

Holly looked from the broken flagpole to the nightdress. When she'd agreed to be a camp counsellor, she had not signed up for ghosts and unexplained accidents. The others started to leave, drifting off to check on their charges, but Holly waited behind and scooped sand over the fire. She wanted to give Emma some privacy at their cabin while she said goodnight to Ismail. It might take him a while to calm her down.

"It's been cut," Grayson said.

Holly snapped out of her daze and focused on him. Grayson was crouching next to the broken flagpole, studying the end.

"Cut?" she repeated.

"Yeah. It's wooden. Look – it's as if it's been sawn most of the way through, but one side is all jagged and splintered where it finally broke."

"So someone has done it on purpose?" Rich squealed, jumping up from his seat. Most of the others had gone, so there were now only four of them left – Rich, Brianna, Grayson and Holly. Brianna pointed at something scattered across the ground.

Rose petals.

"Seems that way, doesn't it?" Grayson said, standing up and brushing his hands on his trousers. "I think we need to show Chad. Make him take this seriously. The flagpole would have knocked Emma out cold, or worse – but imagine if it happened earlier. What if it had hit one of the kids? It would have been serious."

"You're right." Brianna nodded and Holly spotted the rosary beads in her hand. She was clutching them so hard her knuckles had turned white. "We can't let anything happen to the littles. We should go to Chad now, before he goes to bed."

"OK. I can carry it, but it's pretty heavy," Grayson said. "It'd be great if you opened the doors for me." Brianna nodded and Grayson pointed at Rich. "You should go to bed. You'll need plenty of rest after what happened to you today. And, Holly, you might want to check on your kids."

"I can come with you. Emma has gone in—" Holly was cut off by three sets of raised eyebrows. She followed Grayson's gaze and saw Emma was still crying by the side of the cabin. "Oh." She turned back to Grayson and Brianna. "Good luck with Chad."

"Thanks."

Holly watched them leave, said goodnight to Rich and crept past Emma and Ismail. She grabbed her shower stuff and made sure all the kids were breathing on her way to the bathroom. It wasn't too messy in the main room. Yet.

She pushed aside the hollow feeling in the pit of her stomach. What if something happened to her next? Including the snakes in Grayson's bed, there had been three incidents now. Maybe she should go home. Holly shook her head. No, she had to stay. She needed the money if she wanted to go on the Year 13 trip to Paris – that had been the deal with her parents. If she could pay, she could go, end of story.

Holly stepped into the shower cubicle. It would all be fine. She just needed to stay positive.

Tomorrow would be a better day.

CHAPTER 8

"That's it! You've got this!" Holly shouted. "Find a foothold and push yourself up. Press close to the wall – it will help your arms hurt less."

She was leaning slightly over the top of the craggy rocks. A climbing anchor had been driven into the ground behind her to hold Holly in place. A red-haired girl in a blue helmet was climbing the rock face, her ropes attached to Holly through a belay device. Holly pulled the slack from the ropes up every time the girl climbed part of the wall, the taut rope keeping her safe as she scrambled towards the top.

The girl huffed but did as she was told. Within seconds, Holly was pulling her over the ledge. Emma cheered from below.

"Yes!" Holly shouted, holding a hand out for a high five. The girl slapped her palm and Holly unclipped her, giving her a little nudge away from the edge. "I know you were scared, but you did it! Go and sit with everyone else while I help Emma up, then we can have a snack."

"OK," the girl said. She walked over to the group sitting on the grass. "I did it!" she shouted, raising her fists in the air. They all cheered as she joined them, chattering and comparing stories.

Holly waited as Emma fed her ropes up to her. It was a clear, sunny day, so Holly could see for miles from up here. True, it was mostly treetops, but in the distance she could make out the twinkle of the sea. For a second she thought of Dorothea on the Widow's Walk, looking out to the ocean, then she shook her head. She didn't believe in ghost stories.

Holly turned her attention back to the drop in front of her. It was only about ten metres, but that was huge for the kids. The sun glinted off the metal spikes that had been driven into the rock to make footholds and handholds for the kids to grab.

Holly had been climbing for a couple of years now and had her own cute climbing shoes and everything, so she had ignored the spikes on the way up, seeking out her own way on the jagged rock. There had been plenty of natural places to grip while Emma watched from below. Now all the kids were up, it was Holly's turn to make sure Emma joined them safely. Then they'd have a snack before they walked back to the main site for the next activity.

"Ready?" Holly called.

Emma tugged at her ropes and gave the thumbs up before finding a set of spikes. She started to haul herself up.

Holly's mind drifted slightly and she glanced towards the house. You couldn't see much of it from here as the trees were in full bloom, but the Widow's Walk peeked out between a forest of green leaves. She suppressed a shudder and looked down again. Emma was almost halfway up. Holly tightened her ropes.

"Nearly there," she called.

Emma didn't reply, just climbed steadily, moving one foot up, then a hand, the other foot, the other hand, over and over again until she was almost at the top. Holly was surprised that the other girl was so organised when climbing, considering how messy she was in their cabin.

Holly kept tightening the rope, making sure there was no slack if Emma slipped.

Emma wrapped her hand around the last spike, briefly shifting all of her weight onto one foot.

The foothold snapped.

Emma's body jolted suddenly and Holly was dragged forward a few steps. Holly quickly came to her senses and leaned all her weight back, digging her heels into the ground. She stopped still, the anchor she had set up earlier continuing to hold her in place. She breathed a sigh of relief as she felt Emma's weight still on the rope. Thank god.

"Emma? You OK?"

"I think so." Emma's shaky voice travelled up on the wind. "The foothold, it just snapped. I need to get both of my feet on the spikes again. Give me a sec."

"Take your time," Holly grunted. She tightened the rope as much as possible and leaned back, her knees bent. She felt Emma's weight lessen when she put both feet back on the rock face and sighed in relief. Her palms were sweating. She wasn't sure she'd have been able to hold her for much longer and the thought made her feel sick. Holly almost cried tears of joy when a hand appeared over the edge in front of her.

"That was cl—" Emma said, but her face changed from relief to horror as a ripping sound filled the air. Holly heard the girls calling out behind her, but she couldn't tear her eyes away from Emma. The rope between them had started to unravel, threads fraying wildly from a cut that Holly was certain hadn't been there when she'd checked earlier. There were only two sets of the yellow adult ropes. She would have noticed.

Holly tried to loosen it, to reduce the tension on the rope, but her fingers fumbled as she panicked. She gave up and tried to throw herself at Emma instead, tried to grab hold of the other girl's hand and drag her away from the edge, but the anchor held Holly frozen in place. She couldn't reach her.

The rope snapped.

"No!" Holly yelled as she flew backwards, Emma's weight no longer on the rope. She wasn't sure who screamed as she unclipped her harness. Finally free of the anchor, she scrambled to the edge, hoping to see Emma clinging to the metal spikes.

Instead she saw her lying on the craggy rocks ten metres below, her eyes staring up at the sky. Emma's body lay on top of a scattering of red rose petals that had not been there before, her neck bent at an unnatural angle.

The campers started to scream.

CHAPTER 9

Holly hadn't known anyone who had died before. How was she supposed to act? She felt numb. Surely she should be crying, screaming? Sick? Especially because the incident kept replaying on a loop in her head.

They were in the Great Hall now, thanks to an unexpected downpour that had forced them inside. Holly remembered a term from English, "pathetic fallacy", which means when the weather mimics the mood. How appropriate.

She glanced around the long table at the other counsellors. Ismail had been distraught and now sat quietly with Grayson. He wouldn't speak to anyone else yet. Everyone looked exhausted and Holly couldn't blame them – she certainly was. It had been heartbreaking trying to soothe the girls from her cabin before their parents came to collect them. Holly had done her best to look after them, but it was so awful. How would these kids get over something like that?

How would she?

"They're all gone," Chad said as he sat down heavily. He looked washed out as he gestured to the kitchen staff to start laying out food. Ismail folded his arms on the table and put his face in them, obviously trying to tune out the whispers. Looking after the kids had kept Holly distracted, but now they'd gone home she felt close to breaking point.

"Did you see the roses?" Ava said.

"What do you mean?" Fionn whispered.

"When Emma … her body … was put in the ambulance, there were rose petals," Ava explained. "They were stuck in her hair."

"Shut up!" Ismail screamed into the table.

The room fell silent as they all looked at him. Tears were soaked into the sleeves of his hoodie. He opened his mouth again but only a sob came out. Grayson put an arm around Ismail as he cried.

"Dinner's ready," a voice called from the serving hatch at the back of the hall. "I'll leave it all out. Me and the other staff are heading home now. Help yourselves."

Holly was grateful for the interruption. The smell of melted cheese drifted over and her stomach rumbled despite everything. How the hell could she be hungry right now?

"Thanks, Chef," Chad called. He turned back to the group. "I know it's probably the last thing you want to do, but you should eat. It's been a long day and you'll sleep better with something warm inside of you." He walked up to the hatch and slowly people started to go after him. Holly blindly followed, filled a plate with food and sat down again.

It was eerie, having dinner like this, especially after last night, when it had been full of kids and laughter. Tonight everyone ate without even making eye contact.

Most people had stopped pushing food around their plates by the time Chad spoke up.

"OK, everyone, this is the deal." He cleared his throat as they all looked up. "I spoke to the police after they interviewed you all and they're happy for everyone to leave. But the last train today has gone, so I've organised transport for you in the morning. If you haven't called your parents, do it after dinner. I sent out a message to your emergency contacts, but I'm sure they'll want to hear from you."

"OK," Holly said, hesitating for a second, thinking about her empty bedroom in the cabin. "Can I … can I move rooms then? I don't want to be on my own."

"Of course."

"You can stay with us, if that's OK with you, Ava?" Brianna said kindly.

"Sure." Ava shrugged.

"Actually, why don't we all stay together?" Rich suggested through sniffles. "We could use the kids' bunkbeds. It's only for one night."

A murmur of agreement went around the table.

"Everyone can stay in our cabin," Brianna suggested. "I can change the sheets on the kids' beds. Can we, Chad?"

"Sure thing. Just be … sensible, you know?"

"What do you mean?" Brianna asked, her eyes so wide with innocence that Holly almost laughed.

Fionn snorted from the end of the table. "He means no Camp Miller babies."

Chad flushed red.

"Ewww!" Ava squealed, and a ripple of nervous laughter followed. At least it broke the tension and people started chatting again.

"OK, OK," Chad said, and even he laughed, then held up his hands to quiet them down. "I know it's early, but I think you should go and get yourselves packed for tomorrow. I've sent everyone else home for the night, so I'll do the washing-up if you dump your plates in the kitchen for me." Chad sighed and Holly felt for him. This place was his dream and look what had happened. She wondered if he'd ever be able to open again.

"You don't have to clear up for us," Grayson said, but Chad cut him off.

"I know. But I need some processing time and so do you. Just ... talk to each other. Look after each other. Have a moment of silence for Emma and her family. We can regroup here for breakfast and if you need me, I'll be in my office, probably for the night. I have a lot to do." He stood up and collected his tray. "Come on now."

Holly stood up and carried her plate to the kitchen. She knew she was moving on autopilot. She hoped it lasted until she got home tomorrow, then her siblings could look after her for once. She'd give anything to cuddle them now. As she left the kitchen, she saw Grayson waiting for her.

"You OK?" he asked.

"No."

"You will be," Grayson said. He held out a hand and Holly folded her fingers around his gratefully.

He didn't let go until she went back into her cabin to pack.

CHAPTER 10

Holly watched the rest of the group from a distance. She didn't have the energy to join in right now.

"Bagsy the top bunk," she heard Grayson say as he nudged Ismail gently. The poor guy was a wreck, but he smiled grimly at Grayson's comment.

"Bro, you're twice the size of me," Ismail replied, rolling his sleeping bag out onto the floor to join the others. "I don't trust a kid's bunkbed to keep you from squashing me."

Grayson unrolled his own sleeping bag. "Fair. I'll take the bottom then."

"Thank you."

"Is everyone here now?" Brianna interrupted. She had been running around as if they were her new group of kids. Only now did she seem to be settling down.

Holly counted heads and hesitated before nodding. "Yeah ... seven of us."

No one said anything.

"What shall we do then?" Brianna asked. She sat cross-legged on a pillow. Her hair was out of its usual ponytail and hung damp around her face, and she was dressed in red tartan pyjamas. Holly looked down at her own pink sweatshirt and leggings. They were all wearing various cosy outfits because of the damp evening. They looked like kids at a sleepover.

Brianna cleared her throat and continued, "It's only eight thirty, and I don't know about you all, but I don't think I'll sleep anytime soon. We have some board games and stuff if you want to play?"

"Maybe," Holly said as she chewed on a fingernail.

"There *is* something else we could do," Ava said.

"Like what? Truth or dare?" Fionn asked. They were the only one not on the floor, lying on the closest bottom bunk instead.

"No." Ava took a deep breath and fiddled with the little pink stone in her hand. "I think we should hold a seance."

"A what?!" Brianna squealed as the counsellors erupted with protests.

Holly was horrified. "We can't do that!"

"Yes we can," Fionn said, their eyes glittering as they slid onto the floor. They scootched up next to Rich, who nodded in agreement.

"I think that's the best idea I've heard all week," he agreed, linking arms with Fionn. "We can ask Emma what really happened."

"That is so inappropriate," Brianna hissed. "You can't just go holding a seance for your own amusement – it's dangerous. The Bible says—"

"Jesus Christ." Fionn said each syllable slowly. "Do *not* get me started on the Bible."

"Stop!" Holly yelled, her voice cracking. "Stop arguing." She looked at Fionn. "I don't want to contact Emma. I saw what happened to her – I was there."

"But we weren't." It was Ismail who spoke up. Holly couldn't tell if he wanted to cry or hit something. "You said the rope snapped," he said, "but how do we know you're telling the truth?"

Holly's blood ran cold. Was Ismail accusing her?

"What are you trying to say?" Grayson growled, taking Holly by surprise. She hadn't heard him talk to Ismail like that before. "Holly tried her best to save Emma. The equipment was faulty. It's Camp Miller's fault, not hers."

Holly looked at him gratefully. "Except … I don't think it was," she murmured.

"What do you mean?" Grayson asked.

"I checked it all and set everything up after breakfast while the kids were in the cabin getting ready with Emma. I've climbed loads of times; I knew what I was doing. But the gear was left unattended while I went back to the campsite to collect the kids. It took ages to get the girls from our cabin together, so someone had at least half an hour to head out there and tamper with the ropes."

"Are you serious?" Fionn asked.

"Yes, I am. Nothing has happened by accident since we got here, has it?" Holly said. "The snakes in Grayson's bed, Rich getting trapped in the kayak, the flagpole being cut, Emma ..." Holly tailed off, her voice thick.

"So you're saying one of us is responsible? Or Chad?" Rich asked.

Holly shrugged. "I don't know. Maybe."

"So you *do* want to hold a seance?" Brianna said, her hands clasped together again.

"I don't think it will do any harm. Maybe we could ask *her*," Grayson said, shrugging.

Holly sighed. She knew what was coming next. She just hadn't imagined it would be Grayson making the suggestion.

"Who?" Ava whispered.

"Isn't it obvious?" Fionn said, and Holly wondered when everyone had suddenly climbed aboard the ghost train. "Hit the lights, Rich. We're going to talk to Dorothea."

CHAPTER 11

"Oh yes," Rich shrieked.

Holly groaned as Rich wriggled himself up to standing and ran to the light switch next to the door. "I love this idea," he went on. "In my opinion, we all need a little fun after everything that has happened. And yes, I can say that, because of what happened to me." Rich put a hand on his hip and plunged the room into darkness.

"I'm not doing it," Brianna said. "I will *not* mess with the occult!" It was still light outside, but the curtains were closed and the door was shut. The main room of the cabin was dark enough that Holly had to really concentrate on where she was looking. She heard the door to the counsellors' bedroom open and shut as Brianna removed herself.

"I guess that makes six?" Grayson asked.

Ismail grumbled, but he didn't move.

Holly shielded her eyes as Rich pulled a torch from his bag, switched it on and held it to his chin.

"It's showtime. I'm in," Rich said, smiling in the torchlight.

"Me too," said Fionn.

"Rich, do you still have the nightgown?" Ava asked. "It would be useful to have something of Dorothea's. It might help us make contact with her."

"It's in my bag," Rich said. He left the circle briefly, taking the torch with him. The light bobbed and flashed in the corner as he searched his belongings.

"Well?" Ava said impatiently.

"It's ... not here," Rich said. "I swear I packed it earlier. I was going to take it to Chad, but ... it's gone."

Holly shivered as Rich re-joined the circle but told herself not to be ridiculous. There was no such thing as ghosts.

"You must have left the nightgown in your cabin," Ava said. "Never mind. Let's try anyway. Everyone ready?"

Holly gave in and mumbled her agreement. It wasn't like she would have to do anything, and she definitely wasn't going off on her own. Rich placed the torch in the middle of the circle. He balanced it on the flat end so the light pointed at the ceiling. "Instead of a candle," he explained.

"Oh, good idea," Ava said. "It's a shame we don't have one of Dorothea's roses – that would help too."

"Erm, has anyone ever done this before?" Grayson asked.

"I have," Ava replied.

Of course she had. Holly hadn't spoken to Ava much, but she seemed keen to stir things up tonight.

"How many times?" she asked.

"A few." Ava didn't offer any more detail, just brushed her long fringe out of her eyes. "I can start if you want?" She sounded serious.

"OK," they all agreed.

All eyes were on Ava now. Holly could barely see her face, but the torchlight made her eyes seem even more hollowed out. She realised Ava always looked tired.

"We need to hold hands," Ava began.

Holly held hers out. Fionn's cool fingers enclosed her hand on the right, Ismail's tentative ones on the left.

"Now, close your eyes and think about who we want to contact," Ava continued.

"Dorothea," Grayson said loudly.

"Good! You start us off then. You just ask her to come and talk to us, give us some sort of sign that she's here," Ava explained. "But don't let go of each other's hands until we've told her to leave. That's really important. Whatever happens, *don't break the circle.*"

Holly's palms grew clammy as the others joined hands and completed the circle.

"Erm, are you there, Dorothea?" Grayson started.

Rich sighed loudly. "That won't work. Here, I'll do it. Dorothea, we wish to speak with you."

He dragged her name out, like a child imitating a ghost. "If you are here, can you give us a sign?"

Silence. The muscles in Holly's back and shoulders were tense. Knotted. Rich spoke again.

"Dorothea, if you are doing this, give us a— Oh!"

The torch in the centre of the circle fell to the ground with a crash, the light flashing across the room.

"Don't break the circle! Rich, it's working. Carry on!" Ava's voice was louder than the gasps from everyone else.

Holly flinched, grasping Ismail's hand as he almost pulled it away. She didn't think she believed in this stuff, but she wasn't taking any chances.

"Uh, thank you, Dorothea. Is it you doing all this? Are you angry?" Rich said.

The room fell silent again and Holly could hear her own breathing.

"If you are, tell us," Rich continued. "We'll go home. We'll tell Chad and ..."

"I can't do this. I don't know what I was thinking," Ismail interrupted. He sounded angry now.

"We have to carry on," Ava urged. "Even if it's just to end safely."

"OK, I can do that," Rich said. "Dorothea, if you're here, give us another sign. Otherwise, respectfully, we will close the circle."

Nothing.

"Goodbye, Doroth—"

A blood-curdling scream filled the room, causing Ismail to yank his hand from Holly's and dart over to the light switch.

"I told you, no more!" Ismail yelled, tears in his eyes. "Emma is *dead*, and one of you is screwing around. It's not *fair*. I liked her ..." He broke off with a sob.

"Ismail, it wasn't one of us." Grayson stared at the door that led to the counsellors' bedroom. "It came from in there."

"Brianna," Holly said. She was already on her feet, but Ava beat her to the door, the rest of the group trailing behind.

The bedroom was darker than Holly thought it would be, grey clouds filling the uncovered windows. "Brianna?"

"I'm here," came a muffled voice from under the covers. Brianna peered out. "I ... I saw something."

"What?" Ava elbowed her way into the room. "What did you see?"

"A ... a woman. Well, kind of. She was there." Brianna held a shaking hand up to the window. "Her hair was hanging over her face." Her breath caught in a sob. "Her skin was all stretched, her mouth was black ... rotten, all hanging open. She didn't ... have ... eyes." Brianna broke down in tears and Holly perched on the edge of the bed, wrapping her arms around her.

Grayson walked over to peer through the glass, out into the woods. "Here?"

Brianna nodded, her chest heaving.

"I can't see anything."

"It was her," Ava whispered, looking around for Rich.

"Dorothea," he whispered.

"Stop it," Holly warned before turning her attention back to Brianna. "Could you have fallen asleep?"

"I don't know. Maybe," Brianna mumbled.

"That's all it was," Holly soothed. "Just a dream. It's been a long day for all of us."

"But it was so real," Brianna said. "She had the white nightgown on and her hands pressed against the window. Like she was trying to get in."

"I warned you not to break the circle!" Ava said, hugging herself. "It was Dorothea, giving her sign. She's seeking revenge, just like in the story, and now she's loose. We didn't banish her before we dropped hands."

"Stop it!" Ismail kicked the thin wooden door and let out a pained yell. "Just shut up, will you?"

"Hey, calm down, man," Grayson said, and tried to guide him away from the door. Holly was grateful – Ismail was close to losing it.

"No. I'm done. I'm going home." Ismail flung the main door open and they watched him leave.

"I should go after him," Grayson sighed. "He's my roommate. Maybe I can get him to go and talk to Chad or something."

"Good idea," Holly said. "But come back soon, OK? I know it was probably nothing, but it's getting dark out there. Here, I'll get you a torch."

Ava sat with Brianna as Holly and Rich followed Grayson into the main bedroom.

"Thanks. Where's Fionn?" Grayson frowned, taking the torch from Holly and looking at the empty beds.

"Not sure," Rich answered. He sat down on a bunk and picked up a glossy magazine. "Why?"

"I was gonna ask them to come with me. I think they have a phone that's working. Ismail might feel better if he calls home," Grayson said.

"You want me to come?" Holly asked.

"No, you should stay with Brianna," Grayson said. "I'll be fine on my own."

"I'll come with you," Rich volunteered. "We can look for Ismail and Fionn, and I want to get another magazine from my room. I've read this one like five times already."

"Yeah, OK, that would be good." Grayson waited as Rich slid his feet into flip-flops and stood up with a catlike stretch.

"Wait, I'll come too. I feel bad," Ava said, emerging from her bedroom. "Holly, you'll stay with Brianna, right?"

"Sure."

"OK. We won't be long," Grayson said to Holly.

She forced a smile. "We'll set up a nice boring game of Monopoly or something for when you get back," she replied.

Holly watched them step out into the night, her skin prickling.

CHAPTER 12

It took half an hour for Brianna to calm down enough to be on her own. Holly left her hiccupping in bed and stepped onto the porch. No one had come back yet and Holly was getting worried.

Rain was falling so heavily she could only see a couple of metres ahead of her at most. The benches around the firepit were pretty much hidden, so it took a second before Holly noticed the dark figure emerging from the side of the cabin. Holly froze, then groaned with relief.

"God, Fionn, you scared me," Holly said. "Where have you been?"

"Talking to my girlfriend."

"Again? Is this really the time?"

"Don't be so judgemental." Fionn clambered up the steps onto the dry porch and squeezed water from their hair.

"I—" Holly began but stopped herself. She *had* been a judgemental cow, hadn't she? She wished she'd been nicer to everyone. Especially Emma. "You're right. I'm sorry, I'm just ..."

"Freaked out?" Fionn said.

"Yeah."

"Me too," Fionn sighed.

"Seriously?" Holly's eyes widened slightly. Fionn always seemed as hard as nails.

"Yep. After what happened with Emma, I just really wanted to talk to my girlfriend, you know?" They held up their phone's lock screen to show Holly a pretty black girl with a nose ring and hair cuffs decorating her long braids. "She was furious I wanted to work away for the whole summer and—"

A low, tormented moan cut them off.

Holly's skin shrank. "What was that?"

"I heard it too," Fionn said, pointing out past the firepit.

A bubble of anxiety formed in Holly's throat.

"Some of the others went over to Ismail's cabin," Holly explained. "Ismail was ... well, he was upset. About Emma." Holly listened carefully, but the only sound now was the rain pounding on the roof.

"That moan didn't sound like someone was just upset though, did it?" Fionn asked. They had turned even paler than usual.

Holly nodded. "More like someone in pain. Do you think one of them is hurt? Should we check?"

Fionn hesitated. "Who's still here?"

"Just Brianna. Grayson, Ava and Rich went after Ismail. Actually, we should check on Brianna."

Holly went back into the cabin and Fionn followed, dripping water onto the floor.

"Where have you been? Fionn, you're soaking!" Brianna said, peeking up from her duvet.

"Never mind that. Get up. We have to check on the others," Fionn snapped.

Holly took a deep breath. "Fionn's right. We think someone might be hurt."

Brianna shrank further under the covers. "If someone's hurt, one of the others will come back for help. Let's just wait here."

"What if they're all hurt?" Holly pressed. "Or what if they split up and don't know what's happened?"

"But what if it's her?" Brianna's voice was small. "What if it's Dorothea?"

"It's not," Fionn sighed, "because she's not real."

"Brianna, I know you're scared, but we have to do this," Holly said.

A tear rolled down Brianna's cheek. "Fine," she said. "But when we get everyone back, no one leaves this cabin again until the morning. Including you." She turned her wet eyes to Fionn.

"I promise," Fionn said.

"Come on then." Holly left the room, trusting the others would follow. The rain lashed down, showing no sign of letting up. "We'll see if they're next door. We should probably check all the cabins, just in case. Hopefully they're all together and just waiting for the rain to stop before heading out again." Holly tried to sound more confident than she felt. She had a horrible feeling this wouldn't end well.

Fionn jogged up the steps of Grayson and Ismail's cabin. A few seconds later, they returned and shook their head. "Nothing."

The three of them walked to the next cabin: Holly's. She headed inside and peeked into the room she had shared with Emma. It looked the same, except for Emma's usually messy bed, which was now stripped and empty. Holly checked the main room and bathroom.

"Nobody in there," Holly said as she walked down the steps from the cabin. The rain was less frenzied now and the air had started to clear a little.

"Let's try my room," Fionn said. They jogged ahead, running up the next set of stairs to the cabin they shared with Rich.

A low moan sounded from inside, but it didn't sound like the one from before.

Fionn did not come out.

Holly shuddered as a cold sense of dread dripped down her spine. She walked faster, Brianna trailing behind her. They ran up the stairs and entered the cabin.

Holly crept closer to the counsellors' bedroom. Fionn was outside their bedroom, frozen, their eyes fixed on the floor. Holly joined them, Brianna bumping into her as she stopped suddenly.

Brianna started screaming.

"Jesus," Holly breathed as she looked at the scene.

The door was propped open by a lifeless figure that lay half in and half out of the room.

It was Rich.

"Is he OK?" Fionn whispered as Brianna ran from the room.

Rich's body was face down on the floor. The feathers of an arrow from the archery course stuck out from beneath him. She nudged him gently with her foot, not knowing what else to do. "Rich?"

Nothing.

"Roll him over," Fionn suggested.

Holly leaned down and pushed, but he didn't budge. "Help me."

Fionn crouched down and together they pushed Rich over. The arrow clattered to the floor, its tip coated with red. Holly's stomach lurched as she saw the blood that drenched his shirt.

They dropped him back to the floor.

"Did you see it?" Fionn breathed in Holly's ear.

"How could I miss it?" Holly said. The image was tattooed to the inside of her eyelids. "Someone shot him with a frigging *arrow*."

"No, that." Fionn pointed to Rich's limp hand, which now lay next to his body.

He was holding a single red rose.

CHAPTER 13

"Ismail?" Holly shouted into the room. She gingerly stepped over Rich's body and her toe kicked something. She bent to retrieve a pink, heart-shaped stone. It was Ava's rose quartz, something she usually carried on her. Why would it be in here? Holly slipped it into her pocket. "Ava? Grayson?" she called out.

Fionn hung back. "I'm going to be sick," they said.

Holly ignored Fionn and scanned the room. Another arrow lay on the floor, but there was no bow. She reached down to touch it, but Fionn grabbed her arm.

"No – there might be prints on it," they said. "Leave it for the police."

"Yeah. I didn't think." Holly shuddered. "Let's get out of here."

They ran for the porch, gasping for air as they got outside. Brianna stood at the bottom of the steps, shaking uncontrollably. "It was you!" she screamed, pointing at Fionn.

"What?" Fionn raised a damp eyebrow. "You don't think I did this?"

"Then where were you?" Brianna demanded, stepping closer to Holly.

"On the phone," Fionn replied, "sneaking off to sort out my pathetic love life like I usually do! I didn't do this. It must have been one of the others."

"Stop arguing!" Holly yelled, her voice hoarse.

Brianna whimpered. "Where are the others? Did you check the rest of the cabin?"

"No," Fionn admitted. "We didn't. Let's check the beds and bathroom."

"Fine," Holly said. She stepped back in, avoiding Rich's body. Brianna stayed outside as Holly followed Fionn into the bathroom.

Nothing.

"You think it's one of the other counsellors doing this?" Fionn said as they returned to Brianna.

"What about Ava?" Holly murmured.

"What do you mean?" Brianna said, her face pale. Holly put an arm around her.

"She's not in there, don't worry," Holly said. "But she is an Olympic archer, right? She could fire an arrow hard enough to kill Rich. And I just found that crystal she carries everywhere on the floor. What if she lost it in a fight with one of the others? What if Ava is hunting us?"

"Oh god," Brianna said. "We have to go and find Chad and call the police. Unless anyone's mobile works? My signal was so bad I just stopped using it. I doubt it's even charged."

Holly shook her head. "Same here."

"Wait! I have mine." Fionn patted their back pockets and pulled out a slim black phone. "Here, I might have a sig ... wait." They frowned, tapping the screen. "It's dead."

"You're soaking," Holly sighed. "Is it waterlogged?"

"I don't know." Fionn looked on the verge of tears.

"Come on." Holly took charge. "We go for Chad or find a landline – whatever we come across first. Brianna has a key to his office, don't you?"

Brianna nodded mutely.

"Good," Holly said. "Come on, let's run for the front door of the house. Just keep your eyes peeled for a psycho with a bow and arrow."

"Or Dorothea," Fionn muttered.

Brianna's eyes almost popped out of her head. "What?" she said.

Holly shot Fionn a filthy look. "We'll explain later," she replied. "Come on, run!"

Holly felt as if she had wings on her feet. They all flew to the main entrance, a rain-soaked blur of panicked gasps, landing in a pile against the door. "Get inside!" Holly instructed.

"We can't," Fionn grunted, leaning into the thick wood. "It's locked."

"Brianna, do you have this key?" Holly said.

Brianna searched the keys on her lanyard. "Yeah, should be this one." She slid a large brass key into the lock with a trembling hand. It twisted easily, causing a loud click. Holly pushed again.

The door didn't budge.

"I ... I don't get it," Brianna muttered, trying the key again. "It worked; it's unlocked."

"Then it's blocked from the other side," Holly muttered. "We need to find another way in."

"The brew room," Fionn said. "There's a door to the main building in there. If the brew room's open, we might be able to get inside that way."

"And if we can't, we can stay there until the morning," Holly added, while trying not to panic. Where were Grayson and Ismail? She couldn't bear the thought that they were hurt too. "Come on. Stay close to the wall but duck down to avoid the windows. Go as fast as you can and don't stop until you're there. OK?"

Holly crouched as low as she could while still being able to run, making sure that her arm grazed the wall as she went. It was a straight run to the end of the building, then around the corner and into the brew room.

Hopefully.

Holly turned the corner. As she ran through the open gate that led to the lake, a flash of white caught her eye.

"Wait," Holly said, stopping. Fionn bumped into her from behind. "What's that?"

"What?" Brianna asked, following Holly's finger. The shape was clearer now, a definite human figure, one with seaweed ropes of black hair hiding its face.

It was wearing the white nightgown.

"Oh, Lord help us," Brianna gasped. "It's Dorothea. It's really her, oh no, oh no, oh— Ouch!"

Fionn had slapped Brianna. "You were getting hysterical," they explained.

Brianna held a hand to her cheek.

"It wasn't hard. You're welcome," Fionn continued.

"Stop it," Holly hissed. "Where has it gone?" Holly glanced back to the fence.

The figure had disappeared.

"I'll close the gate." Brianna fumbled with the keys. "We need to lock in whatever *that* was."

A hand landed on Holly's shoulder and she fought down the scream in her throat. Instead she turned around slowly, half expecting to find the rotting corpse of Dorothea behind her. Tears filled her eyes as she saw who it was.

"Grayson! What happened?" Holly asked. She threw her arms around him and he sagged against her. Pulling back, she studied him – there was an angry red gash above his eye and he was hunched over, clearly unsteady on his feet.

"I don't know." Grayson squeezed his eyes shut. "Ismail wasn't in our cabin, so we split up to look for him. I was checking the woods around the back and ... I think something hit me? When I woke up, I went back to cabin one but it was empty too, so I thought I should find Chad. I was on my way there when I saw you ..." He touched a hand to his head. "I think I'm bleeding ..." Grayson's eyes were unfocused and he slurred his words slightly. Fionn ran over to help steady him.

"Come on, in here," Holly said, tugging at the brew-room door. "It's open ..."

There was a loud, low thumping sound that intensified as Holly pulled open the door. Her next words stuck in her throat.

Inside, Ismail lay on the worktop, his head twisted backwards into the sink. Roses bobbed on the surface of the water and his head had been submerged, floating just beneath the surface. Running water further distorted his blank face and streamed over the cabinets onto the floor.

"Ismail," Holly breathed. Fionn gasped and Holly choked back tears as the thumping noise continued.

"Look," Fionn said. "The wall." Holly tore her eyes away from Ismail and blood-red letters danced in front of her eyes. It took a second to understand what she was seeing.

REVENGE

The word was scrawled on the wall above the sink, half a metre high, dripping onto the counter. Holly tried not to think what had been used to paint the burgundy letters.

"What is that noise?" Holly whispered as the thumping sound mirrored her heartbeat. Their heads turned towards to the large tumble-dryer.

"Should I open it?" Fionn said.

Nobody answered.

Fionn walked over to the dryer and pulled the handle. The noise stopped and the door gently popped open, releasing a warm perfume into the air, along with another smell that Holly didn't want to identify. Several crisp red petals drifted to the floor and whatever was inside thudded to a stop.

Then Ava's bloody arm dropped out.

CHAPTER 14

"Jesus," Fionn said in a choked voice.

Holly's vision was blurry, but she could see the scene in front of them. Ismail's face rippled beneath the water in the sink and Ava had been folded into the machine like laundry, her torso now flopping out. Going by the amount of dried blood that decorated her arms and face, she was dead too.

"We need to get Chad," Holly said. She skirted around Ava's limp arm and tried the door that led to the main house. "Please don't be locked," she muttered.

"Thank god," Grayson said as it opened in her hand. Holly narrowed her eyes at him. He had to pull himself together – she couldn't look after them all.

"Come on," Holly said.

Fionn copied her, staying as far from either body as they could. Grayson started after them, wobbling slightly. Holly guessed his head was bad.

"Wait – is Brianna still outside?" Holly asked, frowning. "She was only meant to be locking the gate. Wait here." She headed for the door.

"Oh no you don't. We are not splitting up again," Fionn said as they dragged Grayson out into the night, following Holly.

"Good idea," Grayson said. They stood still as Holly called for Brianna.

No answer.

Worry crept over Holly.

"The gate's still open," Fionn whispered. "She never locked it."

"So where did she— What was that?" Grayson yelled.

The hairs on Holly's arm raised in painful goosebumps as a scream tore through the thick, humid air.

"Brianna!" she shouted.

"Up there," Fionn said, their head craned back, looking up at the Widow's Walk from their spot by the fence. "She's up there."

Holly forced her feet to move. When she reached Fionn, she looked up too, just in time to see Brianna scream again.

"Brianna! What are you doing?" Holly shouted, the words raw in her throat. "Get down from there!"

"I don't think she wants to be up there," Fionn said as the three of them huddled together.

"She's not alone," Grayson choked out.

Holly's blood ran cold as a dark-haired figure appeared behind Brianna. Moonlight almost made Dorothea's white gown glow as she raised her hands.

"We have to help her," Holly said. She lurched towards the house, blinded by the tears that formed in her eyes. They had to find a way up that tower and fast.

An earth-shaking slap rang in the air.

"No—" Fionn said.

As Fionn sank to their knees, the realisation hit Holly. She turned to look at the others. "Was that ...?"

Grayson nodded. Bile rose in Holly's throat as Fionn let out a wail.

"I'll ... I'll go and check," Grayson said. "See if she needs help."

He peeled himself away and staggered round the corner. Holly's head was spinning as she followed him, stopping when she glimpsed the body on the ground. She turned around and threw up over and over, gasping for breath.

Emma. Rich. Ismail and Ava. Brianna.

All dead.

Which meant they were next.

"Well?" Holly asked Grayson as he reappeared. His face was slack and his body trembled.

"She's ... her head," Grayson managed to say before retching. He grabbed the wall for support as he emptied the contents of his stomach onto the gravel. He gasped, sucking in deep breaths as Fionn climbed to their feet, shaking like a new-born lamb.

"She's really dead?" Holly asked.

Grayson nodded.

"No," Fionn whispered. "This can't be happening."

"Well, it is," Holly said. She was shaking too, but her voice was firm. Strong. "I don't know what's going on, but we really need to stick together now. We need to get to Chad's office. We can go through the kitchen, get some weapons and then barricade ourselves in there."

"Knives won't work on a ghost," Fionn said, their eyes flat. "We should stay here, in the open."

"No way," Holly said. "Look what just happened! We need a phone. But there is a problem. Brianna had the keys."

"These?" Grayson held up the lanyard. The material had once been white and green with a Camp Miller logo on it. Now it was so saturated with blood it was almost black, leaving red streaks on his pale jumper. "I took them."

"Good thinking," Holly said, but her gaze lingered on the lanyard. She didn't want to touch it. "Fionn, are you with us?"

"What choice do I have?" Fionn sighed, their mouth set in a thin line. "Straight there, right?"

"Yes," Holly said. She led the way back inside and across the brew room again, keeping her eyes firmly fixed on the floor. Grayson reached a hand out and she gripped it gratefully, grabbing hold of Fionn too. They held on to each other as they passed through the door and emerged into a cold, dark hallway.

"The kitchen's over here," Holly said, and led them to the right, then left. She tried to memorise the steps in case they had to run back this way. They landed outside two large swinging doors and Holly eased one open, ushering the others inside in front of her. As soon as they were in, they dropped hands and spread out.

"Here," Fionn hissed from next to the large stainless-steel oven. A magnetic strip ran across the wall above, studded with knives like creepy fridge magnets. Fionn pulled one away with a soft pop and turned it over in their hand. "Come on, get one of these and let's go."

Nobody hesitated. Holly selected a long, thin knife. The point looked sharp enough to do some damage if she needed it to. But, like Fionn said, knives didn't work on ghosts. Holly scanned the shelves in case there was anything else useful.

"What are you doing?" Fionn hissed as Grayson pulled a large white tub from the shelf.

"Is that salt?" Holly asked.

"For protection," Grayson said, shrugging. "My mum makes me watch *Supernatural*. If this is a ghost, salt might be more useful than knives. No harm in having both."

"Fair enough," Fionn agreed.

Holly pointed to the door that led to the Great Hall. "We go through the dining hall and then take a right to Chad's office," she said. "I'll go first, if you give me the keys, Grayson. Let's get there fast. Ready? Go!"

Holly nodded, satisfied, as she watched Grayson cradle the pot of salt in one arm, the other hand brandishing the knife in front of him as he walked backwards, in case Dorothea came up behind them.

The building was silent apart from their footsteps and they moved through the Great Hall with ease, emerging into the corridor in seconds. They got to the office and Holly called out.

"Chad?" she said. There was no answer.

Grayson tried to open the door and shook his head. "It's locked. He's not in there."

"Wait here." Holly pawed through the keys on the lanyard, trying not to think about why it was wet or what was staining her fingers. "Which one is the key to Chad's office, does anyone know?"

Silence.

Holly fumbled with the keys, trying each in the lock, her hands shaking.

"Got it," she said as one finally made a snap as loud as a gunshot. "We're in."

"Thank god," Fionn breathed. They piled in on top of one another and Holly locked the door behind them. Fionn reached up to the light switch.

"Don't," Grayson warned, and Fionn dropped their hand. "Keep it dark."

Fionn wandered off as Holly approached the big wooden desk, looking for the landline under piles of paperwork. Out of the corner of her eye she watched Grayson put his knife down and snap the lid off the salt tub, pouring a thick line of salt in front of the door.

"Hey, look at this," Holly said, picking up a framed photo on Chad's desk. "*Camp Forest Park, 1996.* I bet our parents are in here somewhere." Grayson and Fionn joined her. "Yep, there's my mum."

"And that's my dad," said Grayson, pointing at a tall black teenager who had a high-top fade haircut.

"Nice." Fionn smiled. "Wait, is that Chad then?" They leaned closer, looking at a skinny boy with metal braces and thick glasses, his skin red and sore looking. "No way ..."

"Yep. That's me all right." Holly froze as Chad's voice filled the dark room.

She turned around, the metal knife handle feeling slippery in her hand. There was one person they hadn't suspected.

Chad.

"1996. What a year! I was a Lead Counsellor. It was the best summer ever and—"

"What's going on, Chad?" Holly interrupted bluntly. She'd had enough. "Why is everyone dead?"

Chad's face dropped.

"What do you—" Chad began, his open mouth freezing as he let out a gurgle. There was a wet sucking sound and his body convulsed, a thin black line trickling from his mouth. He fell forwards onto the floor.

"Oh god." Holly began to sob. Grayson pulled her close as Fionn squeezed in behind them. The sharpened end of the wooden flagpole stuck out of Chad's back, the flag still wrapped around it, fluttering limply across his bloody shirt.

But that wasn't the worst thing.

A figure stood in the doorway, dripping rainwater onto the wooden floor. Strings of thick black hair hung across her white face, covering everything but her hollow eyes.

Dorothea.

Holly watched, horrified as she opened her mouth and croaked out a single word.

"Surprise."

CHAPTER 15

"You can't come in!" Holly screamed as the ghost inched towards them. "There's salt on the floor!"

"Yeah, that's busy soaking up good old Chad's bodily fluids."

The figure's voice was familiar.

"Rich?" Holly said. "Is that you? What the hell? We thought you were—"

His mouth twitched. "Dead? No." Rich twirled a strand of synthetic hair around his finger. "Just fake blood. A bit of theatre magic."

Holly's jaw dropped. "But Ismail ... and the others ..." she said.

"Oh, he's really dead. They all are! But I knew you wouldn't check me too carefully. All that blood would freak anyone out."

"There was a rose," Holly breathed as she remembered the scene. She looked at Fionn desperately. "We just assumed ..."

Rich hiked up the white nightdress and pulled out his weapon – a small, sharp hatchet. Holly swallowed hard. That could be a problem.

"What are you doing?" Grayson asked, gesturing to Rich with his knife. "Where did you get that?"

"I was chopping wood for the campfire with it the other day," Rich said. "Took a liking to it." He grinned. "Ava didn't like it so much."

Holly thought she was going to be sick again.

"He means *why* are you doing it?" Holly demanded, her voice strained.

"Why what? Dress up as dear, dead Dorothea? I guess you could say I'm just a little bit dramatic." Rich threw his head back and laughed. "Chad was letting me put on that end-of-week play with the kids, so I raided the costume box after Fionn told their little story about Dorothea. I thought it would be fun to spook a few people."

"Not that," Fionn whispered. "The others. Why did you ... kill them?"

"You mean you don't know?" Rich asked.

"Know what? That you're a psychopath?" Holly spat. She immediately regretted it as the expression on Rich's face changed. Hardened.

"Sit down," he snarled.

Nobody moved.

"Sit down!" Rich roared, swinging the hatchet, his eyes bulging.

"OK, OK. Do as he says," Grayson said. He held his hands up and looked at Holly and Fionn.

"And give me your weapons," Rich snapped.

"What? No." Grayson pushed the others back slightly, but Rich was faster. He leaned forward and wrapped his fingers around Fionn's wrist, yanking their arm away from the group. Fionn's knife clattered to the floor.

"Do what I say or I'll slice their head off. Up to you." Rich's voice was ice cold as he pulled Fionn towards him, wrapping one arm around them. He pressed the hatchet to Fionn's throat, just hard enough for the skin to split slightly.

Fionn whimpered as blood trickled down their neck. Holly had never seen Fionn so vulnerable and it shook her. They'd have to cooperate for now, but she *had* to think of a way out.

Rich could not get away with this.

She nudged Grayson and they slid their knives towards Rich. He loosened his grip on Fionn and pushed them away into the far corner.

"Now sit down," Rich said, picking up the framed photograph. "It's story time."

"OK," Holly whispered, tugging Grayson's hand and pulling him to the floor. She tried her best to sit near a row of shelves she had seen earlier, as far from Chad and his desk as they could get. She caught Fionn's eye and nodded to the shelves. Holly hoped that they had understood. She turned her attention back to Rich, who was waving his hatchet at them.

"Excellent. The year was 1996," Rich began. "My mum was nineteen then and she decided she wanted to apply for Camp America. She got in and was shipped over with a few other kids the same age. She was ready for the best summer of her life, but it didn't happen. The others ruined it for her. There were a bunch of other kids there from near where she lived, but get this: they all thought they were *better* than her. She didn't go to the *universities* they did, didn't live in the *nice part of town* like they did. They dismissed her like she was rubbish, but Mum got lumped in with them anyway, because they were all Brits.

"The American counsellors didn't want her and neither did the 'cool' kids, so she ended up alone. They got so fed up with Mum trying to make friends that they drove her out to the woods and left her there overnight to make her own way home. Can you believe how *cruel* that was? It freaked her right out, especially when she saw the signs for bears, and she fell, slicing her face open on a rock. She should have had stitches, but she didn't get to the medical centre in time, so the cut scarred her for life. Every time she looks in the mirror, she's reminded of that night – trust me. I've heard that story a hundred times."

"Our parents did that?" Holly said, glancing at the framed photo.

"Ah, so you found the photo," Rich said. "Chad showed me it on my first day, you know. He was surprised to see me here, since my mum hadn't replied to his invitation for me to be a counsellor."

"But why all this?" Grayson asked. "I mean, you got stuck in the lake. I pulled you out! Did … did you do that to yourself?"

"Duh." Rich walked over to the desk and sat on it, pushing back so his legs dangled over the edge. He tapped the hatchet on the wooden surface. "It was risky, but it meant no one suspected me." He shrugged. "A necessary evil. You took your time though. I could have actually drowned!"

"More's the pity you didn't," Holly mumbled.

"You." Rich pointed the hatchet at her and Holly's skin prickled. "That climbing rope was meant for *you*, not Emma. Your mother was the worst one. It was her idea to leave Mum in the woods. Your mum made her life a misery."

"I … I'm sorry. But I'm not my mum," Holly said. Rich was wrong, there was no way her mum would have done something so mean. "Neither are you. None of us are our parents. You don't need to carry on her hatred."

"Oh, I do. Don't you see? I've gone too far to stop now. Mum lost it years ago. Dad left her and she hated that I was following in her unpopular little footsteps. I used to be terrified when someone didn't invite me to a party. Mum would find out and make me sit in the attic on my own while all the other kids were at the play centre or having cake at someone's house. I tried to be popular, but it never worked. I became a joke and she punished me even more for it. Eventually she ignored me completely.

"Do you know what it's like to live in a house with someone who doesn't care about you? When that person is supposed to care the most about you? I tried everything to get Mum's attention – I caused trouble at school. When that didn't work, I got straight As. I joined the theatre club, got all the lead roles. Do you think she ever came to see me? No. She was too busy drinking bottles of wine and ranting about her mangled face. She hasn't even looked at me since my dad left and I've had enough of it."

"She won't be able to ignore this though, will she?" Fionn said. "She'll have to pay you attention when she sees what you've done for her." Fionn shuffled onto their knees and waved a hand behind their back so Holly could see, but Rich did not. The black eyeliner that usually circled their eyes was long gone, washed away by the rain. Holly patted around on the shelf behind her, seizing the opportunity as Fionn distracted Rich.

"Exactly!" Rich cried. "You get it! I did what my mum never could. She will *finally* be proud of me, and your parents will pay in a way they never thought possible."

"It's genius, really," Fionn agreed, climbing to their feet. "Sick, but genius."

Holly braced herself as Rich narrowed his eyes.

"Now!" Fionn screamed.

Holly raced towards him, the glass paperweight heavy in her hand, but she wasn't fast enough. Rich jumped off the desk, the wig sliding from his head as he darted to the side, swinging the hatchet at her head.

Stars exploded in front of Holly's eyes and her knees buckled. She reached up to touch her head and her fingers came away slick with blood. Panic flooded her body.

"You shouldn't have done that," she heard Grayson say.

Holly looked up through blurry eyes as Grayson wrapped his strong arms around Rich. He bucked and kicked, but Grayson held tight, forcing him into one of the plastic chairs. Fionn grabbed Rich's legs immediately and Holly fought her nausea to join them, pulling a tangle of climbing ropes from the shelf.

Grayson tied Rich's arms behind the chair as Holly and Fionn wrapped the rope around his legs. Holly's hands shook as she fumbled the ropes, trying desperately not to panic as her vision started to blur.

"I knew I should have killed you first this evening, but I just needed you out of the way," Rich spat at Grayson. "I was planning to go back and finish you off later." Rich tried to fight, but it was no use. They'd tied him tight.

"Look how that worked out for you," Grayson snarled behind Rich.

Rich's eyes were wild as he slammed his head back, grinning widely as he made contact with Grayson's face.

CHAPTER 16

"Holly?" Grayson's voice came through the fuzz. Blood had started to trickle into her right eye and her vision was blurred.

"I think he just hit her with the handle," Fionn said. "I reckon she has a concussion though."

Their voice sounded far away. Holly felt like her ears were full of cotton wool.

"We need to get her out of here," Grayson said, looking back at an unconscious Rich. "The prick knocked himself out trying to break my nose. Come on, before he wakes up."

Holly looked at the blood on Grayson's face. "I can't believe he killed all our friends because of mummy issues." She closed her eyes and grimaced.

"There'll be time to process that later. Grayson, call the police so we can get out of here,"

Fionn muttered, sliding under Holly's arm as they helped her stand.

Grayson reached for the landline, glancing down at Chad's body on the floor. "What do we tell them?" he said. "Poor Chad. He just wanted us all to love camp as much as he did."

"Look how that worked out," Fionn mumbled. "Lesson learned – don't do anything nice for people."

"You're a pussycat really," Holly slurred, her one open eye catching Grayson and Fionn share a wry smile.

"Don't tell anyone," Fionn whispered.

The room started to come back into focus as Grayson dialled on the landline, waiting as the operator read him the options.

"Police, ambulance … everything," Grayson said into the phone. "Wait. What's that smell?" The acrid scent of burning filled Holly's nostrils.

"What smell – oh god." Fionn's eyes widened as a small plume of smoke appeared behind the chair Rich was tied to.

"My grand finale," Rich said, twisting his head towards them, smiling.

Holly heard a clatter as Rich dropped something to the floor. A lighter. "Found it in the kitchen. I thought we could *really* make history repeat itself, just like in Fionn's story about Dorothea. We're going to burn this house down."

Grayson shouted into the phone at the operator, "Fire! Camp Miller, at the old Miller House. There's a fire and there are kids inside. Help!" He dropped the handset, fanning the flames that had sprung up between him and the others. "This is spreading too fast. All the paperwork ..."

"Come on!" Holly yelped. She held a hand out to Grayson and the three of them stumbled over Chad's corpse towards the hallway. "We have to get out of here."

"We can't just leave him." Grayson looked back at Rich. His head lolled again – he was unconscious once more.

"Yes, we can," Fionn muttered.

"I'm with Fionn," Holly said. She picked up one of the discarded knives and they ran from the room as fast as they could, heading for the back door.

It was barricaded, a long piece of rope wrapped between the handle and a nearby pillar. It was knotted tight. They weren't getting out this way.

"I forgot this was blocked," Fionn roared.

"He must have tied it shut," Grayson said. "Fionn, hold Holly."

"I'm fine," Holly growled, tugging at the rope desperately. Smoke drifted down the hall, curling and twisting up near the ceiling as flames began to lick the doorway of Chad's office. Holly started to cough, the smoke clogging her lungs.

"Hurry up," Fionn wheezed.

"I've got it," Holly said. Her head might be throbbing, but she had remembered the first rule of every horror movie – don't leave the knife behind. She sawed at the rope with her blade, finally cutting it as the air started to turn grey. She pulled the doors open and fresh air rushed in. Holly gulped it gratefully as they all fell to the ground, sucking in deep breaths.

"Come on," Holly gasped. "We have to get away from these windows."

"Why?" Fionn asked.

A loud explosion answered Fionn's question. It was the window in Chad's office exploding into a million tiny missiles.

"OK then," Grayson said, moving quickly away from the house. Holly and Fionn scrambled after him until they were all out in the open, on the opposite side of the firepit.

They watched the house as it began to burn.

Holly glanced around at the empty cabins, the woods behind them, the burning house. She had never expected camp to end like this.

Was that a flash of white?

"What was that?" she asked the others, but it was gone. She rubbed her dry eyes. Maybe she should be worried about this head injury after all.

"What?" asked Grayson.

"I ... oh, nothing. So, what do we tell the police?" Holly asked as she slumped down on the gravel. "What if they don't believe us?"

"They will. We'll tell them the truth. Apart from, you know ..." Grayson touched his bloody nose gingerly and sat down next to her.

"Apart from what? The fact that we left Rich in there to burn?" Fionn asked.

Holly was distracted by another flash of white over by the lake. Was there someone out there? She rubbed her eyes again and tried to convince herself she was mistaken.

"We thought Rich was already dead," she said. "We saved ourselves." She was amazed that she sounded firm. Unshakable. She didn't feel that way. "We had to leave him. Right?"

"Right," Grayson said. He looked at Fionn. "Do you agree?"

"I guess so," Fionn replied, looking out at the lake, and Holly's blood ran cold.

Had Fionn seen something too?

Sirens began to sound in the distance.

Fionn cleared their throat and shuffled closer to Holly. "That's if the police find Rich inside when they arrive ..."

Acknowledgements

Writing for Barrington Stoke was always a bit of a dream. When I was a teacher, I taught so many reluctant readers and I recommended these gorgeous books over and over again. Thank you so much to my editor, Ailsa Bathgate, who read my earlier work and decided to add a creepy murder book to her list. This process has been such a learning curve, but between your insightful notes and Catherine Coe's language edits, I feel like it's something we can be really proud of. Thanks to Frances Moloney for promoting this book and thanks, as ever, to my agent, Steph Thwaites, and her team at CB.

Thanks to past colleagues who helped keep pupils alive on residentials! This book was partly inspired by a place called Robin Wood, where many fun and happy hours were spent being covered in mud and screaming on the zipline – and that was me, not just the pupils. I did always think it was haunted. Thank you to Amy Goldsmith and Neil Cremin for checking my rusty climbing knowledge and correcting it. Any mistakes are mine. To the real Holly – thanks for horrifying Queen Camilla by telling her *Win Lose Kill Die* was your favourite book. You're awesome!

Thank you as always to my family and friends, especially Loli and Luke. Luke, I know you think I put you at the end because you're the least important, but it's the total opposite. I save the best for last every single time. Love you x

Our books are tested
for children and young people by
children and young people.

Thanks to everyone who consulted on
a manuscript for their time and effort in
helping us to make our books better
for our readers.